The Doughnut Ring

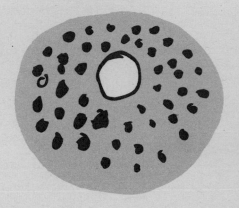

The Doughnut Ring

Alexander McCall Smith

illustrations by Ian Bilbey

BLOOMSBURY

LONDON BERLIN NEW YORK SYDNEY

Bloomsbury Publishing, London, Berlin, New York and Sydney

This edition first published in Great Britain in October 2005
by Bloomsbury Publishing Plc
36 Soho Square, London, W1D 3QY

First published in Great Britain in 1992 by Hamish Hamilton Ltd

A CIP catalogue record of this book is available from the British Library

ISBN 978 0 7475 8056 0

MIX
Paper from
responsible sources
FSC® C018072

3 5 7 9 10 8 6 4 2

Printed in Great Britain by Clays Ltd, St Ives plc, Bungay, Suffolk

www.bloomsbury.com
www.mccallsmithbooks.co.uk

CHAPTER 1

Jim Has an Idea

Jim and his friends all felt very shocked when they heard the news. They liked Mr Pride, the school janitor, and the story of what had happened to him was very sad.

'If I could find the person who stole his car,' said Jim, 'I'd . . . I'd –'

'Steal it back back for him?' interrupted Katie.

'Yes,' said Jim. 'Except it wouldn't be stealing, would it? It would be just taking back what always belonged to Mr Pride.'

Everybody agreed. Mr Pride had been very fond of his car, although it was terribly old and made a dreadful noise. It was a battered old vehicle, half blue and half white, with wheels that looked a bit wobbly. But Mr Pride said it was the best car that he had ever owned, and he would never be able to find one quite like it.

'Can't you buy another one?' asked Jim, as he and his friends stood round Mr Pride in the schoolyard.

The janitor shook his head.

'I don't think I can afford it,' he said. 'I'm going to be retiring soon, and I'm saving my money. I just won't have the cash.'

The more Jim thought about it, the more unfair it seemed. He hoped that the police would be able to find the car and get it back for him, but apparently there was not much chance of that. So Mr Pride would have to do without a car and give up the Saturday afternoon trips into the country which he had always enjoyed so much.

Then, quite without knowing where it came from, Jim had an idea. It was one of those ideas which are so brilliant and so exciting that they have to be announced immediately. Jim did not waste any time. He called together his two best friends, Katie and Mark, and told them what he had in mind.

'Do you think we could do it?' asked Mark hesitantly. 'It's a lot of money.'

Jim nodded. 'You can do anything if you really want to,' he said, not quite sure whether to believe this himself.

'Well,' said Katie, sounding rather doubtful. 'It's all very well saying you're going to organise a sale outside the school each Saturday morning, but what are you going to sell?'

Jim had not thought of that at all, and so he mentioned the first thing that came into his mind.

'Doughnuts,' he said simply. 'Yes, dough-nuts! Everybody likes doughnuts.'

That afternoon, the three of them went to the head teacher, Mrs Craddock, and told her of their plan. She listened carefully, and then, at the end she smiled.

'It's a very, very kind idea,' she said. 'And I'm sure that Mr Pride would be very touched by it. But do you really think it would work?'

Jim nodded. 'We could try it at least,' he said enthusiastically. 'If people knew that the sale was to raise money for a car for Mr Pride, then they'd all come along. I know they would.'

Mrs Craddock nodded. 'He's very popular, isn't he? Yes, I'm sure they'd come.'

She paused to think. Jim thought for a moment that the answer would be no, but then suddenly she smiled.

'Why not?' she said. 'You can try it for one or two Saturdays, and if it works then that's all right.' She paused again. 'But if it doesn't work, then that will have to be the end of it. Do you agree?'

All three of them nodded vigorously.

'Thank you,' said Jim. 'I'll put up a notice and we can have the first sale on Saturday.'

Jim, Mark and Katie began to make their plans. None of them actually knew how to

cook doughnuts, but Jim said that his mother had a recipe. When he told her about why they wanted to make the doughnuts, she was very pleased. She liked Mr Pride too, and she said that the three children could make the doughnuts that Friday in her kitchen, and that she would be happy to do the frying.

It was great fun getting ready. All the ingredients were measured out carefully, the trays dusted with flour (Jim did that) and the mixing bowls and spoons lined up ready for use.

Katie read out the recipe, telling people what to do. Mark did the mixing (until his arms got tired and Katie took over), and Jim moulded the batter into doughnut shapes. Then, when these were carefully laid out on the trays, Mark's mother began to fry the doughnuts.

The smell itself was quite delicious. There's nothing quite like a doughnut smell to get the taste buds working, and by the time they took the doughnuts out of the pan, all three of them could hardly wait to sink their teeth into one.

They had to wait until they were cool, though. Then they all dusted them with sugar and Jim took out one doughnut for testing. He cut it into three equal pieces, and then they were ready. All at the same time they popped the doughnut pieces into their mouths and began to chew.

Delicious! Jim had hardly dared hope that the doughnuts would taste as good as the ones which you could buy in the shops, but these did. In fact, they tasted even better.

'Everybody is going to love these,' said Katie. 'They're going to sell like . . .'

'. . . like hot cakes,' finished Mark.

Jim agreed. He had been rather worried about the success of his great idea, but now he was certain. It was going to work!

CHAPTER 2

Doughnuts for Sale

That Saturday Jim, Katie and Mark were in front of the school well on time. Jim put out the table while Katie and Mark laid the doughnuts on the tablecloth. They had prepared several signs, all saying GREAT DOUGHNUT SALE, and explaining the purpose of the sale. These were displayed in places where people would be sure to spot them.

The school was near some shops, and so there were always lots of people passing by on a Saturday morning. As Jim and his friends stood behind the table, the doughnuts laid out temptingly before them, the first of the morning shoppers appeared.

'Those look good,' said a woman with a red hat. 'May I try one?'

She picked up a doughnut and took a bite from the edge.

'Mmm,' she said. 'That's a good doughnut.'

She bought four. Then, a few minutes later, two children went past and stopped to sniff at the doughnuts. They did not have much money, but they were able to buy one between them, which they split there and then and ate straightaway.

'Very nice,' they said, as they licked the sugar off their fingers.

Now more people arrived. Everybody seemed keen to buy a doughnut, and it was difficult to keep pace with the demand. In fact, after only ten minutes had gone by, they realised that they were going to run out of doughnuts, so popular had they proved to be.

Finally, the last two doughnuts were sold, and with that the sale came to an end. It had taken exactly fifteen minutes to sell every single doughnut.

Jim began to count the money. It added up to quite a sum, and he tucked it safely into the pocket of his jacket. It would take a very long time to save up enough money to buy Mr Pride a car, as even an old car would cost a lot, but at least this was a good start. Even if it took a year, he would still be able to have the car by the time he retired.

Jim had just finished counting the money and was helping to pack away the table and the tablecloth when the trouble began. People who had heard of the doughnut sale were still arriving, and as they arrived they asked where the doughnuts were.

'I'm sorry,' said Katie. 'They're all sold out.'

'But we've come all this way and we expected doughnuts,' said a disappointed voice. 'You can't let us down.'

'But they've all gone,' explained Katie. 'They were so good that everybody bought more than one.'

'Yes,' said Jim, coming to Katie's defence. 'It's not our fault.'

'Yes, it is,' one shopper called out, crossly. 'You should have had enough doughnuts to go round.'

'I'm going to complain to the head teacher,' somebody at the back said. 'You've just wasted everybody's time.'

Jim looked about helplessly. He really thought it was quite unfair that they should be blamed for the fact that the doughnuts sold out. And if somebody complained to Mrs Craddock, then they probably would not be allowed to have the sale again.

And it soon looked as if he was right.

That Monday morning, Mrs Craddock called him to her office. She looked rather severe, and Jim's heart sank at the thought of what she might say.

'I've had a complaint,' she began. 'In fact, there have been two complaints – from very cross people.'

Jim hung his head.

'I'm sorry,' he said. 'All the doughnuts sold out so quickly. We had no idea it would only take fifteen minutes.'

Mrs Craddock nodded.

'I understand that, Jim,' she said. 'I know it wasn't your fault. But the problem is that if you don't have enough doughnuts then you're going to have disappointed people. And you know how people are – they'll blame the school for something like that, even though it's nobody's fault.'

Jim realised that what she said was quite right. But he was very unwilling to give up his idea.

'Give us another chance,' he pleaded. 'We'll get more doughnuts for next Saturday. Please.'

'But how are you going to do that?' asked Mrs Craddock. 'Surely the three of you won't have the time to make all that many more?'

Jim wracked his brains for a solution. Once again, one of his brilliant ideas seemed to float into his head.

'We'll get other people to make some too,' he said. 'We'll have enough. I promise you.'

Mrs Craddock thought for a moment. Then she said, 'One more chance, then. We'll see how things go next Saturday morning.'

Jim thanked her and went off to tell the good news to Katie and Mark.

'That's all very well,' said Katie. 'But who's going to cook more doughnuts? You tell me that!'

Of course Jim had no answer. He thought about it all that day, and he thought about it the next morning too. He asked some of his other friends whether they would make doughnuts for him, but they shook their heads and said no. It wasn't that they did not want to help Mr Pride, it's just that making doughnuts was something they thought they probably could not do.

As he walked home that afternoon, Jim thought that he would probably have to go to Mrs Craddock and tell her that they would call off the next sale. He had promised her that there would be enough doughnuts, but he now thought that it was very unlikely that he would be able to keep his promise.

He stopped in his tracks. He had had another brilliant idea! This time, it was even more brilliant than his other ideas.

'Yes,' he said to himself. 'What a marvellous idea!'

Wheeling round, he raced over to Katie's house.

Katie had not been expecting him. She set aside her homework and listened to Jim as he explained his idea to her.

'A chain letter?' she said. 'What's that?'

'Well,' said Jim. 'I've never actually seen one, but what people do is write to somebody else and ask them to write to another person. And then these people each write to more people, and so it goes on. Eventually hundreds and hundreds of people end up writing letters.'

'It sounds rather silly,' said Katie. 'I don't see the point. And anyway, what's it got to do with doughnuts?'

Jim grinned. Then, his voice lowered, he explained more of his idea.

'We each write to one other person and ask them to send us a few doughnuts. That won't be hard. And they won't mind doing it if they know it's for a good cause. Then they each write to another person and they ask them to send some doughnuts. And so it goes on. Eventually we should have enough doughnuts.'

Katie listened to him, her mouth wide open. She had heard Jim come up with some extraordinary ideas before, but this one was surely the most extraordinary.

'But . . .' she said. 'But . . .'

'Please,' said Jim. 'Please let's try. It can't do any harm.'

Katie was not convinced. She wasn't sure chain letters were a good idea.

'Well,' she said, after a while. 'We could try, I suppose.'

'Good,' said Jim. 'Now, where's your writing pad? We must get these letters into the post straightaway.'

CHAPTER 3

Waiting for the Post

It did not take long to write the letters. Katie had an aunt who was a very good cook; she wrote to her. Jim wrote to a friend of his mother's, who lived on the other side of town, and then he wrote to his older cousin as well. He wasn't quite sure whether the cousin would help, but there was always a chance.

Our school janitor's car has been stolen, the letters said. *We are trying to raise money to help him buy another one, and so we are having a doughnut sale every Saturday. Please could you help us by making some doughnuts and bringing them as soon as you can? If you can't bring them, then perhaps you can send them. Then, could you write to another person you think may help and ask them to do the same?*

After that, the letters were addressed and Jim put them in the post as he walked home.

'I do hope it works!' he said to himself as the letters disappeared through the slot of the post box.

The letters were posted on Tuesday. It was too early for anything to happen on Wednesday, but by Thursday morning Jim was already beginning to worry. When he came home from school that day, he asked his mother whether anything had been delivered for him, but she shook her head.

'What are you expecting?' she asked inquisitively.

'Oh, just a few doughnuts,' Jim replied.

Then he told her about the plan. She looked very doubtful.

'It won't work,' she said. 'Chain letters never work. People just think they're too silly.'

'I know they are,' said Jim. 'But this one isn't. It's for a very good cause.'

'We'll see,' said his mother. 'But in the meantime, we had better make some doughnuts for Saturday. You can't rely on any doughnuts coming out of thin air!'

So Jim and his mother made the same amount of doughnuts as they had all made the previous week. The doughnuts looked and smelled every bit as delicious as the previous ones had, but Jim knew that there would never be enough to satisfy everybody who turned up at the sale.

Friday morning came, and Jim anxiously awaited the arrival of the postman.

'Any parcels for me?' he enquired as the postman brought the mail to the front door.

'Sorry,' said the postman, looking at a list. 'Nothing here for you. What are you waiting for?'

'Doughnuts,' said Jim sadly. 'Lots and lots of doughnuts.'

The postman laughed. 'Just the sort of parcel I like to deliver,' he joked. 'Well, I hope they arrive soon!'

At school that day, Jim told Katie and Mark the bad news. The other two had not been expecting to receive anything, as the letters had all given Jim's address. They were both most disappointed.

'Tomorrow will be the last sale,' said Mark. 'There'll be the same sort of trouble and Mrs Craddock will be furious.'

'I know,' said Jim dejectedly.

'There's always tomorrow,' said Katie. 'Remember that people haven't had much time.'

Jim would have liked to have agreed, but he now had no hope at all that any doughnuts would arrive before it was time to start the sale.

'Perhaps we should cancel it now,' Mark suggested. 'We could put up a notice on the front gate of the school. Perhaps that's the best thing to do.'

Both Jim and Katie thought that this was not a good idea. They would go ahead, they said, even if it involved facing more disappointed customers. At least some people would get the doughnuts they wanted, which, after all, was far better than nothing.

The next morning, Jim did not even think about the postman. So he was quite surprised when the doorbell rang and he left his mother to answer.

'Jim!' she called from the hall. 'Parcel for you. Or should I say, parcels!'

Jim rushed out of his room to see the postman standing in the doorway with two large parcels in his arms.

'These are the most delicious-smelling parcels I've delivered for a very long time,' he said, smiling broadly. 'Doughnuts, I'd guess!'

Jim took the parcels gratefully and rushed with them to the kitchen. He gently unwrapped them and took out the plastic bags that were inside. Within the bags, carefully wrapped in greaseproof paper, were doughnuts – dozens of them.

He laid the doughnuts on a tray. They

were marvellous. Some had jam in them, some had almond custard. Some were plain. But they all – every single one of them – looked delicious!

When Katie and Mark arrived at Jim's house, expecting to have to carry only those doughnuts that Jim and his mother had made, they were astonished to see the array that was set out on the kitchen table.

'But there are hundreds,' said Katie. 'Look at them all!'

'Yes,' said Jim. 'Half of them were made by your aunt, and half by my mother's friend.'

'There will definitely be enough for everyone now,' said Mark, who was itching to try one of the doughnuts himself. 'In fact, there'll be far too many.'

He reached out to pick up a particularly mouth-watering doughnut, but Jim caught him by the wrist before he could touch it.

'No,' he said. 'We asked people to make them for Mr Pride, not for us.'

'If there are any left over, you can eat those,' said Jim's mother. 'Nobody would mind that.'

But there weren't any to be left over. Once again, the sale was well attended, and there was a large crowd gathered in front of the school, but the number of doughnuts on sale was exactly right, and at the end of the sale there was not a single one left.

Jim glowed with pride as he told his mother of how well the sale had gone and of how none of the customers had gone away empty-handed.

'I'm very glad to hear it,' she said. 'Because while you were away, something arrived for you. It's in the kitchen.'

Jim was curious to find out what it was. He went straight to the kitchen and looked inside. There, on the table was a large box. Just by sniffing the air, Jim was able to tell what it contained.

Doughnuts!

CHAPTER 4

The Doughnut Deluge

The doughnuts had come from Jim's older cousin, who had dropped them round at the house himself. On top of the box was a note.

Dear Jim, it read. *I was very happy to help you with your doughnut sale. Here are some which I have cooked myself. I have written to two friends, who will most certainly help you. Good luck!*

Jim was delighted. These doughnuts could be put in the fridge and kept until next Saturday's sale. Together with the next batch which he and his mother would make, there would be enough for that week. With his mother's help, he stored all the doughnuts away, taking only the tiniest crumb of one to taste for himself. It was superb!

That afternoon, there was a knock on the door. Jim answered it, to find a delivery man standing outside, holding a box.

'Is your name Jim Hargreaves?' he asked in a business-like voice.

'Yes,' said Jim, eyeing the box. He had a good idea what it contained.

'Delivery for you,' said the man. 'Please sign here.'

Jim signed the receipt and took the box into the kitchen. This time the doughnuts were from somebody he did not know at all. It was from one of the people to whom Katie's aunt had written, and it contained three dozen large doughnuts, all dripping with red jam.

Jim sighed. It was good to get more doughnuts, of course, but the fridge was full. These would have to be put in the freezer, and then unfrozen in time for the next sale. So he and his mother popped them all into bags and tucked them into the freezer.

'I think we'll have some left over next week,' said Jim. 'Perhaps I can give them to people in the class to pass on to their friends.'

'Well, let's hope no more arrive,' said Jim's mother, licking the jam off her fingers. 'We'll have to start putting them in the basement if they do.'

No more doughnuts arrived that day, nor on the following day, which was Sunday. But on Monday, when Jim returned from school, he knew that something was wrong the moment he came in the door.

'I've had enough of these doughnuts!' his mother called out in an exasperated voice. 'Another six batches arrived today. *Six*! This is really going to have to stop.'

Jim made his way down into the basement to see the new doughnuts. They had come from all sorts of people – some delivered by hand, and others through the post. Everybody had written a note with them, saying how they had not broken the chain and had written to more of their friends to ask them to join in. They were all sure that the friends would be happy to help.

Jim did not know what to do. When he had started the chain letter, he had no idea that it would be so effective. But now that he thought about it, he realised that an enormous number of doughnuts could result if everybody got other people to make a batch. It was like a picture of a tree, with roots spreading out below, more numerous and widespread the further away one got from the top. And what would the end be? A thousand doughnuts? Several thousand? Even more?

Jim swallowed hard. Where would he even

begin to put a million doughnuts? He had no idea.

By the time Saturday came round, you could smell the doughnuts throughout the house. Katie and Mark had helped make more posters, which they hoped would attract more people to the sale, but even if many more people came this week, could they possibly hope to sell all the doughnuts which had arrived, and were still arriving?

On Saturday morning, they started very early to take the doughnuts to the sale. They put out extra tables, but even with these, there was not enough room to display them all. And when people came to buy, they were given not only the number they asked for, but six free ones as well. Everybody was delighted with this, and some people even had the cheek to ask whether they could be given their six free ones without buying any doughnuts in the first place.

At the end of the morning, when they had

served their last customer, the exhausted three looked into the last of the boxes to see what was left. There, inside, sticking to the

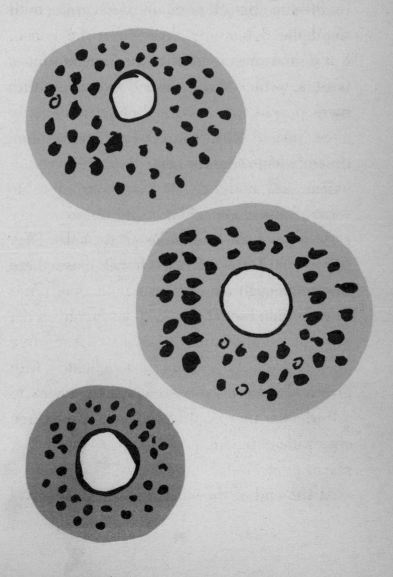

bottom of the box, were three large and succulent-looking doughnuts. They each took one and ate it hungrily. Then, when everything was cleared up, they made their way home.

'I don't want to see another doughnut for at least a week,' Mark said. 'I'm fed up with them.'

'So am I,' said Katie. 'I'm sure I shall dream about them tonight.'

Jim said nothing. He was worried as to what he would see when he got home.

And he had good reason to worry. For there, in front of the house, were the morning's deliveries.

More doughnuts!

CHAPTER 5

Katie Has an Idea

Jim's mother was sitting in the kitchen, her head sunk in her hands.

'We're going to have to do something about all these doughnuts,' she said. 'We can't take any more. I knew this chain letter would get out of hand. You're going to have to write to people and ask them not to send any more.'

Jim scratched his head.

'I wish I could,' he said. 'But I don't know whom to write to. The letters will have been sent all over the place by now. I could never find out where they've gone.'

'But we just can't take more doughnuts,' wailed his mother. 'Where are we going to put them? I had to put ten boxes in the basement this morning. There are doughnuts in my bedroom cupboard and doughnuts under your bed. And that's just from today's deliveries. What on earth is going to happen when more arrive next week?'

Jim could not answer this question. *I shall have to have another brilliant idea*, he told himself. But the trouble with his brilliant ideas was that they did not always come when they were needed.

On Monday, when the postman brought more doughnuts to the front door, Jim asked him to take them back.

'I can't do that,' the postman said, shaking his head. 'That's against the rules. Once a parcel is sent to you, you have to take it.'

Reluctantly, Jim took the parcels in and stacked them in the kitchen. As he stood over them, wondering what to do, a brilliant idea came into his head. He would give the doughnuts away! All he had to do was to put a sign outside the house saying FREE DOUGHNUTS! ENQUIRE WITHIN! All the neighbours would be sure to help themselves.

So the sign went up, and indeed the neighbours took advantage of the offer. Some brought large bags and took away dozens at a time. Others were less greedy, but still took quite a few.

At the end of the day, hundreds of dough-nuts had been given away. The following day, though, fewer people called in for their free doughnuts. Everybody had enough to last them for some time. Unfortunately, on that very day there were twenty more deliveries of doughnuts as the chain letter went further and further afield. This meant that even after giving away so many doughnuts, they were left with as many as they had had in the first place. There just seemed to be no escape!

Jim discussed the problem with Katie and Mark.

'We've bitten off more than we can chew here,' he said. 'Our house is full of doughnuts, and they keep coming in.'

Katie and Mark were silent. They could think of nothing to say, and although they were sorry for Jim, they were both secretly relieved that the doughnuts were going to his house and not to theirs.

Then Katie came up with an idea.

'If we can't sell these doughnuts,' she said. 'Then maybe somebody else could.'

Jim looked at her blankly. 'But we've tried giving them away,' he said. 'We've got too many even to do that. There's nobody left in this town who wants any more doughnuts.'

'There might be somebody,' said Katie. 'Can't you think of who it might be?'

Jim frowned. Who could possibly want to take thousands of doughnuts? Then it dawned on him.

'Do you mean Mr Windram?' he burst out.

'Yes,' said Katie, smiling. 'Mr Wallace Windram, the supermarket king. If anybody can take the doughnuts off our hands, it'll be him.'

Katie's idea was certainly a promising one.

Mr Wallace Windram was the best-known and richest person for miles around. He lived in a large house at the edge of town, and it was from here that he managed the great business that he had built up single-handed. Throughout the country you would see his supermarkets, massive, barn-like buildings, filled to the brim with tasty food.

'If he agrees to take our doughnuts and sell them in his shops, our problem will be solved,' said Jim. 'What a marvellous idea!'

Katie blushed. Everybody was so used to Jim having brilliant ideas, it was good to have one oneself – just for a change! And anyway, look where his brilliant ideas had landed them – in the middle of a mountain of doughnuts, that's where!

CHAPTER 6

Mr Windram, Supermarket King

Everybody knew where Mr Windram lived, but it seemed that nobody had ever met him or knew anybody who had.

'I've seen his picture in the newspapers,' said Mark. 'You see him opening things or presenting prizes.'

'I know,' said Katie. 'But how do we actually get to see him?'

'Phone him,' said Jim, in the voice that he used to express his brilliant ideas.

'But will he be in the telephone directory?' asked Mark. 'Very important people sometimes don't have their numbers listed.'

'We only have to look,' said Jim, as he got up to fetch a copy of the directory.

They paged through the directory until they reached the place in the W's where Mr Windram's name should be. And there it was, with an ordinary number, just like anybody else's. They voted to decide who should make the call, and both Katie and Mark voted for Jim. So, his heart in his mouth, Jim picked up the receiver and dialled the number.

A rather unfriendly voice answered at the other end.

'Mr Windram's residence,' it said.

'Could I speak to Mr Windram?' asked Jim, trying to make his voice sound as grown-up as he could. But all it did was to make him sound rather as if he had a cold.

'Why do you want to speak to Mr Windram?' asked the voice icily. 'Does he know you?'

'Not exactly,' said Jim. 'In fact, not at all. It's about . . . er, a business matter.'

'Then you can speak to me,' cut in the voice. 'I handle all that sort of thing.'

Jim paused. He was sure that this person, whoever he was, would not be in the slightest bit interested in doughnuts. And he was right. The unfriendly voice said no, and then repeated his no, and that was it. Jim heard the telephone wires hum into the distance as the receiver was slammed down at the other end.

'No luck,' he said to the others. 'I don't think it's going to be easy to speak to Mr Windram.'

Jim pondered over the problem of how he could see Mr Windram. It was clearly going to be impossible to speak to him on the telephone, and somebody else was bound to open his letters for him. So the only thing to do was to see him in person – if he spoke to him, Jim was sure that he could persuade Mr Windram to buy all the doughnuts from him. Home-made doughnuts were far, far more delicious than any doughnuts you could buy in the shops. And for some reason, Mr Windram's shops themselves never sold doughnuts.

There was not a moment to lose. Every day, with every delivery of the mail, more boxes of doughnuts arrived at the house. Jim's mother was becoming desperate. The rubbish men refused to take them, the neighbours couldn't bear the sight of another doughnut, and even a farmer, who was a friend of Jim's mother, and who had taken some to feed to his pigs, had reported that the pigs were unwilling to eat any more.

'The doughnuts get stuck on their snouts,' he said. 'They don't like it at all!'

That afternoon, Jim packed a small box of the very choicest doughnuts he could find.

Then, checking up on a map of the town, he set off for the street in which Mr Windram lived. It was a long cycle ride, and he was tired by the time he reached it, but there at last was the high wall behind which Mr Windram's house lay. Now all that he had to do was to get inside.

He parked his bicycle at the end of the street and began to walk towards Mr Windram's gate. It was a very impressive gate – tall and ornate – not the sort of gate one could walk up to and open by oneself. As he got closer, Jim saw that something was going on.

Cars were driving up towards the gate and being ushered in by a uniformed gatekeeper. It was difficult for Jim to know exactly what was happening, but it seemed as if Mr Windram must be having some sort of party. Certainly all the people in the cars were smartly dressed, and faintly, from the other side of the wall, Jim thought he could hear the strains of a band playing.

Jim's heart sank. He had chosen the worst possible afternoon to try to see Mr Windram. How could he possibly see him if he was in the middle of holding a large party for all his important friends? His spirits lowered, Jim walked on past the gates. He imagined what was happening at home now. More deliveries of doughnuts would be being made, and his poor mother would be frantically searching for somewhere to put them. It was a nightmare.

Then, just as he was about to turn around and make his way back to his bicycle, Jim saw the bough of the tree. The tree itself was inside Mr Windram's garden but the bough overhung the wall. Another brilliant idea was about to come!

CHAPTER 7

Gatecrashing the Party

Jim looked over his shoulder. A large car had just driven through the gates, which had swung shut behind it with a clang. Now there was nobody about, and, without waiting, he leapt up and grabbed the overhanging bough. For a moment or so his fingers scrabbled for a grip, but he soon managed a firm hold and succeeded in hauling himself up on to the bough. After that it was a question of inching slowly forwards until he had crossed the top of the wall and could drop down on the other side.

Jim found himself at the very edge of a long, rolling lawn. In the distance was Mr Windram's mansion, a great, white building with soaring pillars at the front. Along the side of the house, there had been pitched two massive striped tents with open sides. The band was playing in one of these and the other was filled with a long table. This was where the party was taking place.

Jim crouched down and ran for the cover of a cluster of bushes. From the safety of his hiding place he was able to think about what he should do. It was one thing to drop into Mr Windram's garden uninvited; it was quite another thing to get to speak to Mr Windram, wherever he was. Jim imagined that he would be in the second tent, among all his guests, somewhere at the table. But where?

As Jim was studying the scene, something

happened that gave him his chance. One of the waiters who was bringing large silver platters out of the house slipped on something and dropped several puddings over one of the members of the band. There was a shout and a general kerfuffle as the bandsman stood up and tried to wipe cream and custard off his suit. A large red jelly had fallen into his trombone and a trifle was trickling down his sheets of music.

While everybody's attention was focused on this unfortunate scene, Jim dashed forward. Nobody saw him as he darted from bush to bush, and then there he was, hiding in a lavender bush right beside the tent. From the bush it was only a lurch and a wiggle to slip under the table.

Underneath the table, there was a forest of legs, all dressed in expensive clothes. Jim squeezed himself past a pair of gold shoes with tiny, sparkling points. Then, taking great care not to touch anybody, he crept over a pair of ankles dressed in bright pink

socks and a pair of legs in brilliant white silk. Here and there, bits of food had been dropped: a sausage roll, half an egg stuffed with caviar, a piece of thin green asparagus on a stick. There were also some very strange things to be seen. He saw an ankle with a large gold wristwatch on it (how on earth could they tell the time?). He saw a pair of false teeth which somebody must have dropped and then been too shy to look for. It was all very interesting.

But Jim had not come for the sights. He had come to find Mr Windram, and he realised that he must be somewhere very close. But, which of these legs belonged to Mr Windram?

Jim studied the legs. All of them looked as if they could belong to a supermarket king. All of them looked grand, rather rich legs. Then a thought occurred to him: surely the host would be sitting at the top of a long table of guests. Mr Windram was bound to have the best place, from which he could look out on all his guests, and that must be at the top.

Inch by inch, clutching his precious box of doughnuts to his chest, Jim crawled up towards the top of the table. When eventually he reached it, he stopped. There were six legs there, all of which looked roughly the same. There were three people seated at the top, any one of which could be Mr Windram.

For a few minutes, Jim had no idea what to do. If he spoke to the wrong set of legs, then he would be discovered and thrown out before he had the chance to put his case to Mr Windram. So he had to choose the right legs.

Jim edged forward again until he was only a few inches away from the legs. He stared hard at them, trying to decide which pair of shoes looked more expensive than the others. But the shoes all looked much the same.

Then Jim noticed the label. One of the

socks on one of the legs was showing a label. Jim stretched his neck forward and screwed up his eyes to see what the label said. *Wind* . . . the legs moved, and so Jim had to crane his neck to read the label again. *Wind* . . . Yes! *Windram's famous striped socks*, the label said. Jim had heard of them. They were sold at bargain prices near the counters of every Windram's supermarket. No rich person would wear such cheap socks unless he was the person who made them in the first place. Jim knew then that he was looking at the legs of the supermarket king!

CHAPTER 8

The Doughnut Deal

Now came the moment of greatest danger. Very carefully, and very quietly, Jim opened his small box of doughnuts. Then, taking the utmost care, he took out the best doughnut there. It was a large one, with a filling of caramel and whipped cream, and it would have melted the heart of the sternest person.

With the doughnut held gingerly between

his thumb and forefinger, Jim very cautiously pushed aside part of the tablecloth at the side of Mr Windram's legs. Then, reaching up, he slipped the doughnut up on to the table to where he thought it would be at the side of Mr Windram's plate.

Nothing happened. Jim sat quite still, his heart thumping with excitement. Surely Mr Windram could not fail to notice it. But there was nothing – not a single sign to suggest that anything unusual was happening. Then, quite suddenly, there came a strange noise from above. It was a snort of some sort, and it was followed by a rather surprised-sounding voice.

'What on earth is this?' the voice said. 'And where did it come from?'

Another voice, belonging to one of the other pairs of legs, gave a reply.

'It looks a bit like a doughnut,' this voice said. 'I haven't eaten one of those for years.'

'Well,' said Mr Windram's voice. 'It looks quite tasty. I might as well give it a try.'

There was silence for a moment. Jim crossed his fingers, praying that it would work. If it didn't, then it would be the end of all his hopes.

'Mmm,' said Mr Windram. 'Not bad!'

Then a fist thumped down on the table, giving Jim a fright.

'Very good!' roared the voice. 'Waiter! Another of these . . . doughnut things please!'

Jim saw a pair of waiter's legs hovering about behind Mr Windram.

'I'm afraid we don't have any, sir,' he said timidly. 'In fact, I have no idea at all where that one came from.'

'Well, it didn't fall out of the sky!' snapped Mr Windram. 'You must have given it to me.'

'I'm sorry,' said the waiter. 'I didn't.'

'I wonder who did then?' said Mr Windram.

Listening to this made Jim realise that it was time for him to act. Summoning up all his courage he leaned forward and tapped one of Mr Windram's legs.

'I gave it to you, Mr Windram,' he said. 'And I've got some more down here!'

After that, everything happened very quickly. There was a bit of a fuss when Jim was discovered beneath the table, and one of the waiters wanted to throw him out im-

mediately, but he was stopped by Mr Windram.

'If this young man wants to speak to me,' said Mr Windram, 'then let him. Come on, young man, what's all this doughnut business about? You certainly have delicious doughnuts, if I may say so!'

So Jim sat down next to Mr Windram and told him the whole story. At the end, when he had got to the point where he was telling about how he crawled along under the table, Mr Windram began to laugh.

'You must have seen some very odd sights down there,' he guffawed. 'Did you see my brother-in-law's teeth, by the way? He's always losing them at parties.'

Jim nodded, which made Mr Windram laugh all the more. Then, wiping the tears of laughter away with a large silk handkerchief, he returned to the serious question of all the doughnuts.

'So you want me to take these doughnuts off your hands and sell them in my supermarkets?' he asked.

'Yes,' said Jim. 'I'd be very grateful if you could do that.'

Mr Windram narrowed his eyes and stared at Jim.

'And all the money would go to this old janitor . . . Mr Pride?' he asked.

'Yes,' said Jim. 'It would.'

For a moment or two Mr Windram said nothing. Then he smiled and patted Jim on the shoulder.

'Do you want to know what I think?' he asked. 'I think . . . I think it's a very good idea. Yes, a very good idea indeed. Doughnuts? Let's have lots and lots of doughnuts.'

Jim heaved a sigh of relief as Mr Windram went on to say how he would send some of his men round to Jim's house immediately to collect the doughnuts and put them in cold storage.

'Of course, you won't continue to get them for much longer,' said Mr Windram. 'Sooner or later these chain letters stop. But that won't matter. Perhaps you and your mother can make some for me then. And I'll pay you well.'

'Thank you,' he said. 'Thank you, Mr Windram.'

Mr Windram chuckled.

'What about another doughnut?' he said, pointing to a jam-filled one which he had spotted in Jim's box. 'That one will do.'

Mr Windram ate all the rest of the doughnuts in the box. Then, as the guests had by now started to leave, he accompanied Jim to the front gate.

'Come back and see me soon,' he said. And then, as Jim hurried down the road, eager to tell Katie and Mark the wonderful news, the supermarket king called out after him, 'And bring some doughnuts with you!'

'All right,' shouted Jim. 'I will!'

And Jim did. Mr Windram liked the doughnuts, of course, and asked for more, which Jim gave him. Eventually people stopped sending Jim doughnuts, but that didn't really matter. The doughnuts had sold so well in the supermarkets that enough money had been raised to buy Mr Pride a new car – and a very nice one at that. Jim still saw Mr Windram, though, as they had become quite good friends. Mr Windram asked Jim whether he would like to come with him on his inspections of his supermarkets, which Jim readily agreed to do. And after they had finished inspecting a supermarket, they would return to Mr Windram's house for something to eat.

And what did they have to eat? That's right! Doughnuts.